A Collection for Kate

W9-AYF-002

by Barbara deRubertis
Illustrated by Gioia Fiammenghi

Kane Press, Inc.
New York

Book Design/Art Direction: Roberta Pressel

Library of Congress Cataloging-in-Publication Data

DeRubertis, Barbara.
    A collection for Kate/by Barbara deRubertis; illustrated by Gioia Fiammenghi.
      p. cm. — (Math matters. Level 3)
       Summary: As she adds up the items in the collections that some of her classmates bring to school, Kate tries to come up with a collection of her own that has enough items for her to share.
    ISBN-13: 978-1-57565-089-0
    ISBN-10: 1-57565-089-4 (pbk. : alk. paper)
    [1. Collectors and collecting—Fiction. 2. Addition—Fiction. 3. Schools—Fiction.]
     I. Fiammenghi, Gioia, ill. II. Title. III. Series.
PZ7.D4475Co 1999
[E]—dc21
                                                                                              98-51116
                                                                                                   CIP
                                                                                                     AC

10 9 8 7

First published in the United States of America in 1999 by Kane Press, Inc.
Printed in China.

MATH MATTERS is a registered trademark of Kane Press, Inc.

www.kanepress.com

Kate slumped in her seat. She frowned.

Her teacher was giving the class one last reminder. "Next week is collection week. If you signed up to share your collection, be sure to bring it on the right day!"

Kate peeked at the calendar with one
eye. She had signed up for Thursday.
The problem was that she didn't have
a collection. And she had less than
a week to get one. "Oh, brother,"
she muttered under her breath.

Sign-up day had been weeks ago.
Lots of kids had rushed to put their
names on the calendar, so Kate did too.
It had seemed like she would have
PLENTY of time to get a collection.
Not anymore.

Kate spent most of the weekend looking for a collection. She looked through her closet, her drawers, and her junk box. She looked on top of her bookshelves. She looked under her bed.

Kate had a little of this. She had a little of that. But she didn't have a lot of anything. How many of something did she need to make a collection?

She decided to wait and see what the other kids would bring.

On Monday morning, Joseph showed his collection first. He had two tote bags FULL of books. He could hardly carry them all!

"I collect books about reptiles," he said. First he showed 9 books about snakes. Then he showed 5 books about lizards. Kate added them up in her head.

SNAKES OF SOUTH AMERICA

RATTLESNAKES

COBRAS

SNAKES

Pythons

SNAKES OF NORTH AMERICA

GARDEN SNAKES

SNAKE TALES

GIANT SNAKES

"Oh, brother!" she thought. "I don't have 14 of anything.

Next came Emma. She could hardly wait
to show her collection.

"I collect two kinds of magnets," she said.
She had 13 animal magnets, including a
giraffe and a zebra. And she had 11 food
magnets, including a pizza slice and a
cookie with jelly in the middle. The cookie
looked good enough to eat.

Kate wrote down the 13 and the 11.
Now she had to add 2-digit numbers!
She already knew this was going to
be a big sum.

Kate moaned, "I definitely don't
have 24 of anything."

That night Kate searched the house.

She found a little of this—four old books about horses. She found a little of that—five magnets on the refrigerator. But she didn't find a lot of anything.

13

On Tuesday, Ben shared his shell collection. He had three boxes FULL of seashells. The first box held 15 shells from a trip to Florida. The second box held 10 shells from a trip to California. And the third box held 5 shells from his grandmother in Hawaii.

Ben showed all the different kinds of shells. Meanwhile, Kate quickly added up the numbers in her head. They were easy to add: 15 plus 10 equals 25, plus 5 more makes 30.

Thirty! The collections kept getting bigger!
And so did Kate's problem. Sure, she had a
few seashells. But six shells were NOT
enough for a collection.

Joan was next. "She's always such a show-off," thought Kate. "But she only has one box. Maybe. . ."

"My family took a loooong trip last summer," Joan began. "I bought postcards at all the places we visited. We went to LOTS of places. So I have LOTS of postcards in my collection."

19

Joan counted the postcards. Kate thought
she would never stop counting.

Joan had 11 postcards from Colorado,
13 from New Mexico, and 15 from Arizona.

Kate wrote down the numbers. "Hmmm. . .
each of these numbers is bigger than 10,"
she thought. "So the sum must be more
than 30!"

"Thirty-nine!" Kate gulped. "Oh, brother!"
was all she could say.

That night, Kate found two old postcards in a drawer. She found one in between the sofa cushions. And Dad gave her one that had come in the mail. Four postcards. Big deal.

Then Kate put her 6 seashells in a box.
A small box.

"Oh, brother," Kate muttered.

On Wednesday, Rachel shared her pig collection. It was huge! Her mom had to help her carry the six shoe boxes filled with pigs.

The boxes held 10 wood pigs, 12 glass pigs, 16 metal pigs, 4 plastic pigs, and 7 plush pigs. Everyone said, "Wow!" Rachel beamed. But Kate did not.

Kate fussed and fumed. Rachel had so many pigs, Kate had to regroup to find the sum!

Kate stared at the number. "Can that be right?" she wondered. It was such a BIG number! Maybe she had made a mistake.

"I'd better check this sum on my calculator,"
Kate thought. She punched in all the numbers.

There it was again—49.

"I feel sick," she groaned. "I might not be
able to come to school tomorrow. . . ."

That night Kate looked at all the stuff she'd found. She had a little of this. She had a little of that. But she didn't have a lot of anything.

Kate arranged all the little groups on her bed.

She had 4 books about horses.

She had 5 magnets, 6 shells, and 4 postcards.

She had no pigs.

But she did have 3 frogs and 5 teddy bears.

Slowly, Kate began to smile.
"Ah-ha! That's it!" she thought.
Then she quickly packed
up everything on the bed.

At school the next day, Kate set out all her things. Everyone watched. No one said a word.

Finally her teacher spoke. "What is it that you collect, Kate?" she asked.

Kate smiled proudly. "I collect COLLECTIONS!" she said.

"Cool!" "What a great idea!" said the kids.

KATE'S HORSE BOOKS

"Very nice, Kate," said her teacher. "I suppose you didn't want to collect just one kind of thing."

"Right," said Kate. "For me, that just didn't add up!"

Addition Chart

Here are some ways to add.

1. Count on. 5 + 2 = ?

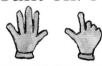

5 and 1 more is 6 and 1 more is 7.

2. Use doubles. 5 + 6 = ?

5 and 5 is 10 and 1 more is 11.

3. Use a related fact. 2 + 8 = ?

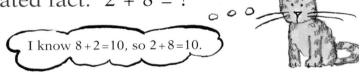

I know 8 + 2 = 10, so 2 + 8 = 10.

4. Skip count.

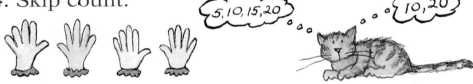

5, 10, 15, 20

10, 20

5. Find and use a pattern.

20 + 10 = 30   70 + 10 = 80   40 + 10 = 50

30 + 20 = 50   40 + 50 = 90   70 + 30 = 100

6. Use this rule to add 2-digit numbers.

First add the ones. Then add the tens.

Regroup when you have ten.

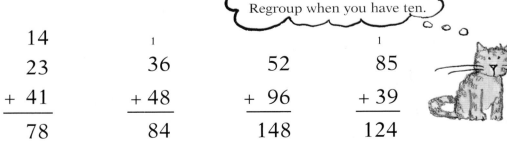

```
  14           1            52           1
  23          36                        85
+ 41        + 48         + 96         + 39
____        ____         ____         ____
  78          84          148          124
```

No regrouping.   Regroup ones.   Regroup tens.   Regroup ones and tens.